THE CLOTHES HORSE
and Other Stories

Janet & Allan Ahlberg

PUFF

PUFFIN BOOKS

Published by the Penguin Group
Penguin Books Ltd, 27 Wrights Lane, London W8 5TZ, England
Penguin Putnam Inc., 375 Hudson Street, New York, New York 10014, USA
Penguin Books Australia Ltd, Ringwood, Victoria, Australia
Penguin Books Canada Ltd, 10 Alcorn Avenue, Toronto, Ontario, Canada M4V 3B2
Penguin Books (NZ) Ltd, Private Bag 102902, NSMC, Auckland, New Zealand

On the World Wide Web at: www.penguin.com

Penguin Books Ltd, Registered Offices: Harmondsworth, Middlesex, England

First published by Viking 1987
Published in Puffin Books 1989
Published in this edition 2000
1 3 5 7 9 10 8 6 4 2

Set in Bembo 16/21pt

Printed in Hong Kong by Midas Printing Ltd

British Library Cataloguing in Publication Data
A CIP catalogue record for this book is available from the British Library

ISBN 0-141-30798-6

Contents

The Clothes Horse

ONCE UPON A TIME a magician made a horse out of clothes. He used two pairs of trousers for the legs, two pairs of shoes for the feet, a mac for the back and a tie for the tail. The head was made from a large sock, with buttons for eyes and a painted mouth. The magician cheated a little with the ears, however. They were cut out of felt and sewn on.

Well, the truth is the horse didn't look too much like a horse, when you got close to him, which I suppose was only to be expected. All the same, he had been put together by a magician, and could therefore gallop and neigh and eat his bag of oats with the best of them.

For a time the horse found himself a job pulling a milkman's cart; this was in the old days, before they had milk-floats. But he soon got bored with this and ran away (galloped away, I should say). The milkman didn't mind too much, however. He was bored with being a milkman. And the magician wasn't bothered either. He was occupied just then making a cat out of bottle tops.

Well, the horse ran away, and – to cut a long

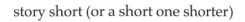

story short (or a short one shorter) – had his trousers stolen by a couple of tramps whose own trousers had worn out. His mac was taken by a little girl who wanted to make a tent with it. His tie was 'borrowed' by a man who couldn't get into a restaurant unless he was wearing one; and his sock was removed by another man (with a wooden leg) who was getting married.

Anyway, by this time there was not too much left of the horse. (There isn't too much left of the story either.) For a little while he did try walking around (or trotting, I should say) in just his shoes. But he only felt silly doing this, and besides it often scared people (dogs, too) to see four shoes coming down the road with nobody in them. They thought it was a ghost – no, *two* ghosts!

So, finally, one bright and sunny morning the horse stepped out of his shoes and completely disappeared. Then he thought to himself: This must be the end of me! And it was.

Well, perhaps not *entirely* the end, if the truth be known. He was still *there* after all; you just couldn't see him. Anyway, what happened later (this is really another story, but I will tell it all the same), what happened later was this: The horse went back to haunt the magician and play tricks on the bottle-top cat. And after *that* he had the clever idea of stealing washing. He stole two pairs of pyjama bottoms, a couple of blankets, another sock, a sun hat . . . and so on. Finally, so I've heard, he got a job on the stage

– pantomimes, mostly. Perhaps you have seen him. Of course, some people think he is really just two men dressed up as a horse. There again, you and I know better, don't we?

Life Savings

THERE WAS ONCE a woman who decided to save parts of her life till later, when she might have more need of them. She had the idea when she was quite young, and her parents encouraged her. The first part of her life she ever saved was half an hour from when she was four. Later, she saved a day from when she was five, another day from when she was five and a half, six days from when she was six . . . and so on, all the way through her life until she was seventy.

Well, she put all these life savings in a safe in her parents' office. (They had a fortune-telling business, with a little magic on the side.) Each one had its own special box with a label giving the duration – that means how long it was – and her age.

Eventually, as I said, the woman got to be seventy and decided to spend some of her savings. First she opened the box with a day in it from when she was eight. Her heart began to pound the moment the box was opened. She lost all interest in the office and the fortune-telling business, and rushed out into the park. Here she played on the swings and rolled on the grass and fished in the pond and ate ice-cream. By the end of the day she

was worn out, but her cheeks were rosy and her eyes shone.

The next morning after breakfast the woman opened the box with a week in it from when she was ten. After that a great deal happened – and a great deal didn't happen. Dusting didn't happen, for instance, or washing-up or making an appointment at the hairdresser's. Not many bills were paid or weeds dug up. At the end of the week the woman needed another week to sort herself out. All the same her step was light as she walked about the town, and her friends said she was a changed woman.

Well, so it continued for some years with the woman spending her savings bit by bit. Not all her experiences were happy, of course; life is not like that. The two days from when she was fourteen, for instance, were dreadful. She felt terribly shy *all* the time and was desperately worried about an almost invisible spot on her chin.

Then, finally, when she had used up all her life savings, the woman took to her bed, read a book for a while and – presently – died.

Some days later when friends were clearing out the office, one box of the woman's savings was discovered unopened. It was tucked away under a pile of old letters in the safe. The woman herself must not have noticed it. Its label (in her father's hand) said: Half an hour, age four.

Well, as soon as the box was opened, odd things began to happen. One of the friends went racing up and down the stairs – the office was on the third floor; another made a den under the desk, and a third played with the phone.

Of course, as you will realize, it was the last half-hour of the woman's life that was causing this. Now that the woman herself was dead, it had nowhere else to go and, apparently, no reason to come to an end. In fact, as far as I know, it's still around . . . somewhere.

So, there we are. If ever you should feel the urge to act like a four-year-old (unless you *are* a four-year-old) you can blame it on the life savings of the woman in the fortune-telling business, with a little magic on the side. That's what I'd do.

The Jack Pot

THERE WAS ONCE a giant who had a problem with boys named Jack. Just because their name *was* Jack, these boys all thought it would be *no* problem to rob the giant, or slay him even (some of them were quite bloodthirsty), or otherwise make a nuisance of themselves in the house – pestering his wife, for instance. Each day the unhappy giant would find these little scamps hiding behind the milk bottles on the front step, or peeping out of his slippers in the sitting-room (not all of them were clever). Once he even found one trying to use the phone, for some reason. This was ridiculous, of course. He was too small to dial the number, let alone lift the receiver.

Well, the giant attempted to solve his problem in various

ways. He put up notices saying: 'NO JACKS, JACKS KEEP OUT', and so on. Unfortunately, these boys were not much interested in reading, and anyway not all of them *could* read. They were all ages, you see. Some hadn't started school yet; one of them even crawled in!

The giant also tried 'Jack Powder' and bought a cat. But the powder didn't put them off, it only made them sneeze; and the cat preferred chasing birds to chasing boys. Besides, these particular boys often had little home-made swords with them. The giant tried other methods, but these didn't work either; and all the time the Jacks kept coming. What is worse, a few Jills (even) started showing up, and a Jock, too, as I recall.

Finally, when everything he could think of had failed, the giant came to a decision. Since he could not solve his problem, he would do his best to forget about it. With this in mind, he bought a large

pot and put it in the kitchen next to the fridge. After that, whenever he or his wife or their small (fourteen-foot) son came upon a Jack, they would drop him into the pot and leave him there for a while. Each evening after tea the giant or his wife would stroll down the garden and empty the pot at the far end, which from the Jacks' point of view was about fifteen miles away.

Well, for a time this solution worked . . . well. The giant recovered his peace of mind, and his wife cheered up, too. But something else also happened. You see, by and by the Jacks in the 'Jack Pot' got to know each other, became pals and, eventually,

formed a football team, which has since made quite a name for itself in the local league. However, unfortunately (for the giant) they have not lost their interest in giants. And, of course, as you will probably have spotted, a Jack is one thing; a *team* of Jacks is something else.

Now the giant is plagued with Jacks, twelve at a time (eleven plus a substitute). Often they arrive roped together like climbers, and one way or another they are proving to be most ingenious. The giant is at his wits' end. His wife is threatening to leave him and go to her mother's. The cat has already run away.

So there it is: if you have any clever thoughts on this

subject, there is one giant I know who would be glad to hear from you. His address is:

Mr Biggs,

Beanstalk House,

The High Street.

Perhaps you might drop him a line. (Not if your name is Jack, though.)

No Man's Land

THERE ARE ALL KINDS of lands, as you know. There's Basutoland, where the Basutos live; Scotland, where the Scots live, and Heligoland, where the Heligos live (or maybe *go* to). There's the Land where the Bong Tree grows, and the Happy Land, far, far away. There's Cloud Cuckoo Land. There's the Land flowing with Milk and Honey (and Rice Krispies, too, I hope). And . . . there's No Man's Land.

One day a girl heard about No Man's Land and immediately began to wonder where it was and who lived there. She heard about it on the radio. Actually, she only half-heard about it. She was eating a bag of crisps at the time, and reading a comic.

Well, then the girl asked her mum and dad about No Man's Land,

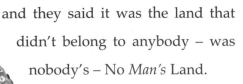

and they said it was the land that didn't belong to anybody – was nobody's – No *Man's* Land.

'It could be No Woman's Land, if you like,' her mother said.

The girl, however, was not satisfied with this answer. So she went down the road to her grandma's house, and asked her.

'No Man's Land is the land where no men live,' said her grandma; 'only women and children.'

'But what about the boys?' said the girl. 'They would grow into men sooner or later.'

'All right . . . women and girls then,' said her grandma.

But the girl still wasn't satisfied. She went further down the road to her Uncle George's house.

'No Man's Land?' said Uncle George. 'I can tell

you about that. I've been there! It's the land where the *No-Men* live.'

'What's a "No-Man"?' said the girl.

'Something that isn't a man,' said Uncle George. Then he became all mysterious and wouldn't say any more; also the phone rang, which he had to answer.

Well, the girl was even less satisfied with this, as you can imagine. After all, *anything* isn't a man (except men . . . and boys, maybe). I mean, a *dog*'s a No-Man, if you believe that – or a carrot, even – or a brick!

So, finally, the girl went right to the very end of the road where her best friend lived.

'No Man's Land? That's easy,' said her friend. She was sitting on her swing. 'It's the land where everybody says, "No".'

'Not even, "No, thank you"?' said the girl.

'No – just "no",' said her friend. 'And all the men are called Noah, and all the women Nola. They have loads of . . . notices all over the place, and the time is always twelve o'clock – noon – get it?'

'And the month is always November!' said the girl.

'That's it – and they all speak Norwegian!'

'And are as nosy as can be!'

'And eat nothing but . . . noodles!'

At that moment the next-door neighbour came into his garden with a deckchair and a portable radio. Shortly after this, the girl heard – or half-heard, for she was eating an apple at the time –

something which put all thoughts of No Man's Land right out of her head.

'Who's "*The Shadow Chancellor*"?' she said.

And her friend – in the up-rush and the down-rush of her swing – said, 'The Shadow Chancellor? . . . That's easy!'

The Night Train

SOME YEARS AGO, when the world was smaller than it is now – and a good deal flatter, come to that – the Night Train brought the night. At the end of each day, it set off with its loads of night – usually in sacks – and delivered them to the four corners of the kingdom. (I should say the world was a good deal *squarer* then, too.) It also carried large numbers of teddies and books of bedtime stories; toothbrushes, hair-rollers and tins of cocoa.

Then, at each station on the line, sacks of night were untied and the night itself rose up and enveloped the town (or village, or whatever). Of course, as you will appreciate, night came somewhat suddenly in those days. One minute you were running up to bowl, say, and the next – bang! – the moon was out. The nights could be patchy, too, and sometimes rather slow to fade away into the following morning. Well, these were disadvantages, certainly, as was the occasional sack of nightmares which the Night Train also carried. However, there were sacks of sweet dreams too, and by and large the inhabitants of the world (the King, the courtiers, the loyal subjects) all found that this arrangement with the Night Train suited them fine.

Then, suddenly, towards the end of a warm spring evening, this happened: The Night Train was held up by a gang of robbers (*dis*loyal subjects, you might call them), who robbed the passengers, kidnapped the driver, and *stole* the night.

A few hours later a ransom note was delivered to the Royal Palace. The King's secretary read it aloud to the King. 'They want a sack of gold for the driver,' she said, 'and half your kingdom for the night.'

'Half my kingdom?' cried the King. 'That's daylight robbery!'

'It's traditional, though,'

his secretary said.

Meanwhile, in both halves of the kingdom there was much yawning and scratching of heads. Night-club owners were looking worried, night-school teachers were twiddling their thumbs, and the palace switchboard was jammed with calls from irate parents unable to get their children off to bed.

Well, the next day – or rather the *same* day, for the sun was still low in the sky – the King called an emergency meeting of the Royal Council together with his Chief of Police.

During the meeting, the Archbishop said, 'I believe the day of reckoning is at hand!'

The Royal Philosopher said, 'The longest day must have an end.' And (a little later), 'Tomorrow is another day!'

The Chief of Police said, 'We are searching for those robbers night and day . . . well, *day* anyway.'

And the King's Doctor said, 'An apple a

day keeps the doctor away,' which was what he usually said.

After the meeting – which reached no useful conclusion – the King continued to discuss the matter with his secretary. Her advice was straightforward. 'Issue a Royal Proclamation,' she said. 'Have it proclaimed throughout the length and breadth of the land.'

'The land's square,' said the King. 'The length and breadth are the same.'

'Don't quibble,' said his secretary. 'Offer half your kingdom –'

'Not that again,' said the King.

'And the hand of your daughter in marriage, to whosoever – '

'I don't *have* a daughter,' said the King. 'I'm not even married!'

'Never mind,' said his secretary firmly. 'It's traditional.'

Now then, whether the King would have taken this advice, I have to confess will never be known. For at this point in the story we have come to a sort of right turn, as it were. You see, it is also traditional in stories involving sacks (ropes and nets, too, I believe) for *mice* to play a part. What invariably happens is, they nibble through the hero's bonds, or the net in which the lion has been captured, or – as in this case – one of the sacks of night piled up in the robbers' hideout.

Well, I've no doubt you can guess what

happened next. For one thing, the hideout was not a hideout for long. Soon, hanging over it like a marker buoy, there was a small patch of dark and starry sky. (The night had poured out of the sack, you see, and escaped up the chimney.)

So then the police surrounded the place; the robbers gave themselves up; the sacks of night were loaded once more onto the Night Train, and life, in hardly any time at all, returned to normal. In the days (or rather nights) that followed, there was once more employment for night-watchmen, overtime for railway-workers and a good night's sleep for anyone who wanted it. There again, those that chose to make a night of it were free to do so; ships that wanted to pass in the night could pass in the night, and things that went *bump* in the night could . . . bump.

So there we are: what else can I tell you? Well, the robbers were sent to jail for a thousand and one nights (and days), and the King in due course married his secretary. They had grown extremely fond of each other, and besides, as the King explained when he proposed, it was traditional.

As for the Night Train, it continued to give good service for many years, until, by and by, the telescope was invented and scientists discovered the movement of the planets. The world, it turned out, wasn't square at all, but round like an orange. Furthermore, it 'rotated on its axis' (whatever that means) every twenty-four hours, causing night to follow day . . . *automatically*. (I may say, quite a few people fell *off* the earth when first they heard how fast it was spinning, and many more went about on their hands and knees for weeks.)

However, progress will not be denied, I

suppose, and sure enough from that time on the Night Train was done for. Now it lies rusting and forgotten in a siding, the King's great-granddaughter rules the land and the *Gravy* Train is all the rage. Of course, it carries rather more than gravy, you understand. I mean, what use is gravy without lamb chops, for instance, and mint sauce, and roast potatoes and peas and baby carrots? And what's a dinner without a pudding: deep-dish apple pie and cinnamon and cream – and what's a pudding without . . . ? But there we are, I'm getting carried away and will be into another story soon, if I don't watch it. 'The longest day must have an end', as the Royal Philosopher said, and the longest story, too, if it comes to that. So, I will stop now, desist, lay down my pen, and call it a day . . . Well, all right, a *'night'* then.

God Knows

O NCE – I will not say 'upon a time', for there was no time then, only eternity – the Children of God (there were three of them) climbed onto their Father's knee and demanded a story.

'Isn't it your Mother's turn?' said God.

'No,' said the children. 'Yours!'

So then, reluctantly, God put aside His newspaper, rubbed His chin, and began. 'Once upon a time (*He* could say that, of course; He was God) there was a place called . . . Mars.'

'We've had that already,' said the children, and they pointed through the open window to a small red planet hanging low in the night sky.

'Jupiter then,' said God.

'And that!'

'Earth?' said God.

'No,' said the children; 'not had that,' and they smiled and snuggled closer together in happy expectation of what was to come.

'Well,' said God, 'once there was a place called Earth.'

As He spoke, a third planet (complete with moon) took up its position in the sky beside Jupiter and Mars – and the History of the World began.

'In the beginning,' said God, 'not a lot happened; just earthquakes – volcanoes – dust storms, that sort of thing. The atmosphere was full of ammonia and methane gas.' ('Ugh!' said the children.) 'It was pretty hot, and pretty boring. Then, after a while, the seas formed and the grass began to grow.'

Up in the sky the Earth was turning green and blue, with swirls of white cloud trailed around it, and patches of white snow at the poles.

'Did the seas have fosh in them?' said the children.

' "Fish",' said God. 'Yes, by and by. And later there were . . . seals and frogs and turtles and

alligators and antelopes and sabre-toothed tigers and
. . . people.'

'No dinosaurs?' said the children. 'You had
dinosaurs on Jupiter.'

'All right, dinosaurs, too,' said God. 'Only they
became extinct after a time, and the people took
over.'

Above them in the sky, the dinosaurs were taking
leave of the Earth and preparing to become fossils.
God paused for a moment and blew His nose.

'And after that things speeded up a little. There
were the Pyramids and the Great Wall of China; the
Battle of Hastings and the Boston Tea Party. And
there was the Domesday Book and the Invention of
Printing and Mozart and Charles Dickens and the
Beatles.'

'What else did they invent?' said the children.
'We like the inventions.'

'Well, let's see,' said God. 'Bicycles – zip-fasteners

– cheese – boats and planes . . . *spaceships!* They went to the Moon.'

Now the dark side of the Earth was glittering with city lights, and a silver spaceship hung in the sky between the Earth and the Moon.

'Did they go to Mars, too?' said the children.

'By and by,' said God.

Just then a voice called from the kitchen. 'Supper's ready!'

God got to His feet with the children still in His arms. 'Good heavens!' He cried. 'Is that the time?'

After that – and when they had kissed their Mother, of course – He hurried them upstairs to bed.

On the stairs, the youngest child said, 'Do they have duncing on the Earth?'

' "Dancing",' said God. 'Oh, yes!'

And the oldest said, 'I'm going to make my own

place up, one of these days. I'm going to call it . . . Pluto!'

And the middle one laughed at Pluto. 'What a name!'

God tucked them in and moved to pull the curtains across.

'Leave them open!' said the children. 'We want to look at the Earth.'

As He reached the door, the children did their best to make Him stay. 'Don't go!' they said. 'What else did they invent? What happens next?'

But God was not to be fooled. He knew what they were up to. 'What happens next?' He paused and rubbed His chin. (Meanwhile, above them in the starry sky the Earth hung, waiting.)

'God knows,' said God
– and went downstairs.